Copyright @2020 by Michael Neno

All rights reserved. No part of this book may be reproduced in any form or by any electronic or mechanical means, including information storage and retrieval systems, without permission in writing from the publisher, except by reviewers, who may quote brief passages in a review.

This publication contains the opinions and ideas of its author. It is intended to provide helpful and informative material on the subjects addressed in the publication. The author and publisher specifically disclaim all responsibility for any liability, loss or risk, personal or otherwise, which is incurred as a consequence, directly or indirectly, of the use and application of any of the contents of this book.

WORKBOOK PRESS LLC
187 E Warm Springs Rd,
Suite B285, Las Vegas, NV 89119, USA

Website: https://workbookpress.com/
Hotline: 1-888-818-4856
Email: admin@workbookpress.com

Ordering Information:
Quantity sales. Special discounts are available on quantity purchases by corporations, associations, and others. For details, contact the publisher at the address above.

ISBN-13:   978-1-954753-30-3 (Paperback Version)
              978-1-954753-31-0 (Digital Version)

REV. DATE: 11.02.2021

THE CHILDRENS MAGICAL ADVENTURES

MICHAEL NENO

WORKBOOK PRESS
RECOMMENDED
LITERARY BOOK COMPETITION 2021

CONTENTS

Adventure One—The Rescue · · · · · · · · · · · · · · · · · · 07

Adventure Two Saving Bernie · · · · · · · · · · · · · · · 34

Adventure Three Castle hope · · · · · · · · · · · · · · 42

Adventure Four Finding Mrs. West · · · · · · · · · · · 52

Adventure One–The Rescue

Many many years ago imagination and magic would combine to make children's lives wondrous, happy and filled with adventures but all to soon they would be forgotten with growing up, but during these special years' magical things could happen if only you only believed

It was the year of 1915 that a young married couple living in the city of London in England decided to move into the countryside. This was because the man Kenneth Ingle wanted a good place for his three young children to grow up, and to escape the hustle and bustle of city life during the Great War that was turning lives upside down all over the world. An educated man experienced in property sells and with a limited knowledge with legal matters. Gloria his wife was an extremely happy housewife and devoted mother who was never so contented than whilst caring for her children. Having made the decision to move as a family it was left to Kenneth to find a suitable home for them. Being well travelled around the country it did not take too long to find a house set in its own grounds on the edge of a small market town of Newton Priory. Being under the age of 13 the children's lives were soon filled by exploring the lightly wooded area close to the end of the large nicely grassed garden behind their new home, separated by a granite stone wall with a trellis archway covered with a climbing rose with red flowers.

For nine–year–old Asa, this was like a doorway into a magical world full of adventure, whereas for the girls Kaya aged eleven and Jade, the oldest at thirteen years, it was a place where they could talk to the animals and be as a princess in their own wonderland. Whilst in this wondrous place, none of the children was concerned by the raging fighting of world war one or the trauma of the dreaded telegram carrying news of the loss of a family member or loved one. For their mummy and daddy just everyday life was a constant struggle hence their father Kenneth had joined the army so as to provide the family with a regular income.

Things were just about perfect until one wet and windy day while they were playing in their bedrooms, dressing up in the assorted costumes that had been discovered hidden in a large wooden trunk in the attic when the family first moved into their new home. Everything was shattered by the sound of a woman screaming which they recognized immediately as being their mother Gloria. They had only ever heard their mother as upset as she was now once before, that being the day that their grandfather passed away having been battling typhoid contracted while working as a ships carpenter overseas. Normally a sprightly and proud lady of only 35years with shoulder length, wavy, strawberry blonde hair and a warm happy smile on her face, always ready to play with her children and tell them stories which she made up just for them. Without the slightest hesitation all three children rushed down the narrow wooden staircase and into the lounge door to see if their mother needed any help. As they entered into the lounge to their mother they were stopped by the strong arms of a large burly man in a military uniform. These all three children knew meant bad news had been delivered about their father who had been serving in the army as a soldier for the previous three months. Never before had they ever seen their mother without a smile on her face but today she was just curled up on the floor crying. Jade immediately sensed that all was not well so she took the other children by their hand saying, "Mummy needs to be alone so we had better go and leave her for a while" Before leaving Asa pulled away from his sister and ran over to his mother handing her a fresh tissue before turning to walk slowly out of the room.

Returning to the girls' bedroom all three children where

obviously upset and worried about their mother and by not being able to help her. The two girls trying to hold back their tears, clinging to the teddy's that mum and dad had given them for Christmas only a matter of months previously, while young Asa occupied his mind looking through one of the picture story book that were already there when they had come to live there. None of them knew what had happened, none the less they knew something bad must have happened with their father. "I wish we knew what's happened. That way we could help mummy." said Kaya in a state of frustration. "We'll be told all about it soon my little sis." responded Jade as she hugged Kaya comforting her. They had been there for a couple of hours when Asa suddenly jumped to his feet still holding the old book that he was reading saying in an excitable voice, "That's it I know what to do. It's all here." Surprised his sisters looked up and enquired as to what he was talking about. "It's right here. All we have to do is read this magic spell aloud under the full moon at midnight." Not really believing him the girls just went along with Asa if only to humor him.

At a few minutes before midnight all three children carefully crept down the stairs avoiding any of the creaky ones and out of the kitchen door into the back yard. As luck would have it there was not a single cloud in the sky on this night and more than this it was a night with a full moon shining brightly as if it were a ball of fire. Opening the book Asa flicked through the pages until he reached the one that he was looking for. Looking firstly at Jade who was carrying a picture of their daddy and then at Kaya, Asa started to read out the printed spell before him. "Look around with eyes that see, bring this person back to, me so mote it be." Neither girls believing that Asa's magic spell would work held back from expressing their doubts from their brother as he obviously felt like his idea would help.

The following morning whilst Jade was doing her best to act as mother to her younger sister and brother by providing a bowl of porridge for breakfast Gloria entered the dining room taking a seat at the end of the large oak table where meals where ate. Asking the children to sit down she took a deep breath before speaking, "The man who came yesterday has informed me that your daddy has been captured by the Huns and is a prisoner. That means that he will not be home again yet and we will not have many things." Now they all knew what had happened to upset their mother so badly. Both girls obviously started crying but little Asa stood up and placed his arms around his mother's neck said, "Well that means I'm the man of the house now and I got to look after you now for daddy." "We will be okay my children as long as we never forget daddy loves us all very much and wants to come home to us."

With the previous days' rain and gales subsided the sun was now shining and starting to dry up Gloria sent the children outside to play so as to write a few letters to her family informing them of the news about her husband, private Kenneth ingle. Sealing the last envelope, she raised her eyes to see the large family photograph that hung on the wall above the open stone fireplace, where she and her husband would often sit on the floor playing cards during the cold and dark winters evenings before the beginning of the war that was taking so many young men away from their loved ones. Looking through the window she could see her children sitting on the wooden garden bench looking ever so sad and she felt her eyes fill with tears with a feeling of helplessness at the sight.

Suddenly Asa jumped to his feet suggesting the three of them go into the wooded area to search for their daddy to whom the girls reluctantly agreed even though they knew that their daddy was not there but wanting to give him something to feel helpful with. As they entered through the archway into the woods there was a bright flash of light that came from nowhere and filled the area all around them, like the glare of lightening, but it was a bright sunny day with no clouds to be seen which had them all surprised by its occurrence. Was the source of light just a freak of nature or was there a reason for it happening then and there.

Nothing was any different so Asa looked all around deciding on the best direction to go with their search. To the left was a narrow footpath bordered with ferns on both side and a few young saplings with a large oak tree. Straight ahead was a steep slope with thick bramble bushes over growing the smaller plants and large rocks that protruded from the earth leading up to tall fir trees that lined the ridge. To the right was a wider earth footpath that winded its way through a mass of brambles, nettles and creeper vines to a wooden gate that opened into the small field where the girls often played and stroked the wild rabbits that would come up to them without the slightest fear or hesitation along with a couple of field mice that often emerged out of their hiding place with no fear of them.

"Let's climb to the top." suggested Asa pointing to the ridge in front of them, so the girls sluggishly followed him. Picking up a stick half the thickness of his arm and the length of their grandfather's walking stick Asa started swinging at the brambles trying to make a walkway through like an explorer did in the hot thick jungles of Africa, but the girls were distracted by picking and eating the blackberries that grew on the brambles.

They had been struggling up the slope for about 35 minutes when a low squeaky voice greeted them by saying "Good morning. Where are you going?" Stopping dead in their tracks the children looked all around them but could not see anyone. Again they heard the low squeaky voice, "Down here. I'm down here." Looking down their eyes were greeted by the sight of the small head of a red squirrel looking up at them and wearing what appeared to be a white coat and purple hat. "Mr. and Mrs. Field mouse asked me to watch out for you. It was Kaya who, surprised and astounded, was the first to speak and ask the obvious question, "Why can we hear what you are saying, animals can't talk? "We 've had the ability for many years but kept it secret because humans are not ready for this knowledge. Your great king Arthur knew a magician called Merlin who cast a spell to help us understand your kind. Since then only a few young humans have ever had the ability to talk with us."

Brushing down the front of her straight white full length dress fashioned by her mother out of a discarded curtain that had once hung over the window in the bedroom of their old home Jade enquired, "Why have you waited to talk to us when Kaya and I have been talking to you for ages and ages?" the squirrel ran up the side of the nearby Fir tree, stopping on a small branch and stated that they wanted to before now, but Merlin 's spell prevented it, but after they had performed the spell everything would become clear to only them. The wise old owl that lived nearby had told him to bring them to him so he could explain everything. Asa who had been relatively quiet came up with the idea that they return home until the following morning because he was getting hungry and didn 't 't want mother telling them off for being late in. Quickly arrangements were made to meet Sammy in the morning and to go to meet the Owl, plus all three children had to swear to never telling any other person of what they had discovered that day.

Nice and early the following morning which was a Tuesday all three children came rushing down the stairs and into the kitchen for their breakfast, trying not to show the obvious excitement at the looming meeting with the wise old owl. Gloria, sensing that her children where keeping something hidden from her, calmly sat at the breakfast table cupping her chin in her palms looked first at Jade the eldest and then at Kaya and Asa before asking as to what they were going to be doing that day. Kaya was about to reveal their plans when the sharp feeling of Asa 's foot kicking her ankle altered what she said to, "Nothing mummy, We're only going to the woods to find some blackberries to pick and some flowers for you."

Meanwhile Bernie and Dora field mouse where on their way to the large tree stump at the bottom of the slope in the wooded area where the children often climbed in play, when Sammy the squirrel came down from the tree branch he was sat on to great them. Dora was looking much the typical mother figure dressed in a matronly style dress with a little blue bonnet and small Black Hand bag tucked over her shoulder while Bernie was wearing a brown workman corduroy style jacket. Referring to the grand old owl he announced, "Ollie is waiting for you and where are the children?" Wiping her hands down the front of her face Dora looked up at Sammy and assured him that the children were on their way, whilst Bernie was fearful that the children had told of their secret and the animals would be captured and put into cages for show." I hope those children haven't told anyone about our secret. They will haunt us down and capture us if the humans get to know we can talk to them." Bernie hesitantly announced "Don't worry about the children, we can trust them." assured Dora. Before long Sammy, Bernie and Dora were met by the children, all dressed, prepared and anticipating what lay ahead of them with a mixture of excitement and uncertainty.

Setting off toward the old stone barn to meet Ollie the owl, they were joined first by Bernard the badger, who was dressed in a thick khaki top and also by Samuel the seagull wearing a blue and white sailor type shirt. Bernard introduced himself and Samuel who had a very French accent. Samuel said that he couldn't stay with them because Ollie wanted him to do something for him, but would see them again later before flying up into the sky and heading off in the direction of the coast. It was Jade that began to dampen the original excitement by proclaiming, "I don't think we should go too far from home for too long in case our mummy needs us." to which

Sammy reassured them all by saying "Merlin's spell makes time stand still while you are with us so it will be as if you had 't been anywhere." Reaching the gateway to the small field that housed, at the far end, an old stone barn, Asa briefly admitted being a bit scared because he had never been so far from home without his mother or father, but both Jade and Kaya offered to hold his hand as they walked. Whoever had told them about time standing still there was to be proved true later that day by the fact that Gloria asked why they had all come back home so soon after leaving.

The children reached the barn filled with confidence at meeting Ollie and were greeted with the sight of him sitting on a high wooden beam, holding a newspaper with his wings. "They're here Ollie like I said they would be." announced Sammy confidently. Looking up from his paper and peering over the top of a pair of bifocal spectacles, Ollie stated that he had seen them coming as soon as they had entered the field. After the introductions were done, Kaya turned to Ollie and asked outright if any help in finding their father could be given by the animals. "Yes. We are already doing what we can young lady" which had feeling a bit flattered at being called a young lady, replied Ollie sitting tall and official on a ledge up above all the others present in the barn. Pulling his fob watch out of his waist coat pocket, Ollie checked the time then announces that he was expecting a visit at any time from Samuel the seagull with important news as to private Ingle and his location.

Squawk Squawk signaled the sound of the arrival of Samuel back from where he had been, hopefully baring the news being awaited by Ollie. "I found him! "Said Samuel excitedly "He and other prisoners are in Bruggebin, in Belgium but I believe they are about to be moved. This news needed some thinking about by Ollie so he advised the children to return home until he was ready so reluctantly they left. Having to return home all three children were feeling a mixture of frustration and anticipation at their recent news discovery about their father.

For two days there was no contact and the girls began believing that everything that had happened previously, must have been some sort of shared dream born out of missing their daddy so much, but Asa refused to think this and insisted to his sisters that they keep faith in Ollie. Looking through the large lounge window down over the freshly mowed lawn toward the archway into the magical world beyond, Asa turned to his sisters and said in a disappointed way, "Look you two, Ollie told us that he would contact us when he had any news about dad so please don't give up now, maybe they can't contact us unless we are in the woods. "Come on.". "I don't want to go, I'm busy!" snapped Kaya aggressively who was occupied reading a book, agreed with Asa so the three of them headed off to go out. Gloria was busy in the kitchen preparing an evening meal shouted out to them not to be long because their evening meal would be ready in another hour. Asa rushed across the lawn followed by Jade with Kaya bringing up the rear in a sluggish way mumbling under her breath about having to go out, but it wouldn't be long before she was to change her mind.

As they entered the wooded area through the archway at the bottom of the garden they again experienced the bright flash of light and giving them a tingling all over their bodies like static electricity. In a fraction of a second it was gone and they were once again in a different world where magic was. As if by magic they were soon greeted by Bernie and Dora who had been awaiting their arrival. "We are so happy you have come today, Ollie told us to watch out for you and bring you to him." said Bernie pleased with himself. At the same time down and to their right, came the sound of rustling from a small thistle bush before scurrying away into a tuft of grass, which was shown to be a hedgehog that did not appear any different in the same way as their new friends Ollie, Sammy and the others. This had Kaya who, no longer reluctant to be there, confused asking why this was so. It was Dora that settled Kaya's curiosity by explaining how Merlin was only able to put the magic spell onto a few animals and all the rest had not changed in any way. Focusing their minds on the impending meeting with Ollie and the hoped for good news as to their father, all three children offered to carry Bernie and Dora so as to arrive at the barn sooner which was surprisingly accepted. Whilst Dora was very carefully picked up by Jade and held in her open hands, Bernie opted to travel in Asa's jacked pocket amid the buttons, piece of string, marbles and sweet wrappers that little boys carried.

It was not long until the children were standing outside of the rear of the old barn eagerly waiting to hear the news that Ollie had acquired. Dora who had been carefully placed on the ground along with Bernie placed down by Asa clambered under the old rackety barn door before the children entered, joining them. An eerie creek came from the door, as Jade slowly pushed it open, leading into a large spacious building with only an old broken down tractor and no longer used livestock pens. Looking all around they could not see Ollie at first but out of a dark indentation high up above them he came, carrying his newspaper in one wing and a cup of tea in the other." Good. They brought you like I told them." he said with a masterful and commanding voice which Bernie and Dora acknowledged. Taking a deep breath Ollie began to convey his news to the children which had their full attention as he spoke. "You should thank Samuel for flying all the way across the channel to see Philippe for information about your father. He and his soldier comrades are being marched to the coast before being taken on a ship to a German prison camp.". "No!" cried out Kaya "We have to rescue him and bring daddy home to us". Pushing his bifocals up on his nose and dropping the newspaper he was reading, Ollie looked directly at Kaya and said in a reassuring voice, "Do not concern yourself young lady even as we speak plans are being put into place to help your father return home to you and your mother. I'm only awaiting some important news that Samuel has gone back for and will bring back from Philippe" "Where is he." enquired Asa.

At that moment, as if by demand, the unmistakable sound of Samuel's squawk could be heard drawing closer through the sky. Coming through the hole in the unrepaired roof, Samuel landed on the top of the old tractor bathed in the bright beam of light shining through onto it. Exhausted from his long journey across the English Channel, before straightening himself up and addressing Ollie, he relayed the news which they had been waiting for before turning to the children and especially Jade, telling her that he would need her help very soon to write a letter. "But what do I say?" asked Jade doubting her own ability to know the right words, but Ollie was soon able to give her the confidence needed by telling her that he would tell her exactly what to write. With that decided, Ollie suggested that they all go until the next day because he had much to do. So again they departed but this time feeling a lot more positive.

Far away across the sea in Belgium, a group of British prisoner where being marched along a wet and muddy dirt track toward the coast by their German captors, heading for the ship that would take them to a prison camp in Germany. Their clothing was very dirty, wet and streaked with blood as a result of weeks on the western front. Among these tired, hungry men wishing for a hot bath, shave and yearning to be home with their loved ones, was the children's father private Kenneth Ingle holding on dearly to the thoughts of his young wife Gloria and their children. Known as just Ken to his comrades, this brave man was constantly trying to think of ways to escape to get back home, but little did he know that help would be coming from the most unlikely of sources.

It was the Saturday night, not far from their destination, as they were huddled in a group around an open fire, in a field that provided no shelter for them as they tried to sleep, that a very low voice reached Ken's ear. "Take heart. Help will be coming for you, but don't tell anyone." Looking all around himself he could only see his comrades and the silhouettes of the enemy that were guarding them. With the drizzly rain falling and the distant sound of cannon fire in the distance Ken put what he heard down to that but again he heard the quiet whispering voice telling him to keep faith because help was coming but not to say anything not even to his comrades. This time the voice also said, "Watch out for a seagull that will be carrying news." He already knew that carrier pigeons where used by the army to pass messages on and so thought that seagulls were in some way also being used. Why couldn't he tell his buddies? Why was the army only going to rescue him? Or was it a clever scheme by the Hun to fool or trick him. Who knew? But he decided to go along with it for now.

The following morning, back in England, the children were up bright and early, ready and eager to go. Being all too aware of Ollie's needing her to write a letter, Jade first searched her own bedroom before telling Kaya and Asa to keep their mother occupied whilst she finds some paper and a pencil or pen to write with. On this occasion there was no complaint or moaning from Kaya as she knew only to well as to the reason why her sister had instructed her to do this. On this particular day the sun was hidden behind the clouds threatening rain, so before daring to go out the children wrapped themselves up well and wearing their Wellington boots. Gloria couldn't help but wonder as to where they were going to and what they were doing. As they left through the kitchen door she stopped jade asking if they were forgetting about their daddy to which she replied, "Never mummy, he will come home to us soon." With that said Gloria felt more at ease knowing that her lovely children were coping with their circumstances well.

This time the children wasted no time in going straight to the old barn rather than waiting for any of the animals to take them. Very soon they were at the creaky wooden door looking around them before entering. They had barely entered when they were welcomed by the hoot hooting of Ollie as a group of animals were being talked to by Ollie obviously discussing things and making plans. The sound of Samuel's squawk suddenly had all eyes looking up at the hole in the roof as he came through with drops of rain dripping off the tips of his wings, landing on his usual spot on the top of the old tractor before relaying his news. "Bonjour. Contact has been made with private Ingle but he doesn't know who by yet. "announced Samuel.

The drizzly rain that had been falling on Kenneth the night before had moved away westward and was now beginning to fall on the barn and countryside where they were now, but that did not concern the children because as they had a more important thing to do. For Jade she must write the letter that Ollie asked her to whilst the other two children busied themselves in other ways. Asa clambered up onto the driver's seat of the tractor and pretended to drive it while Kaya occupied herself searching for and collecting as many feathers as she could with the intention of using them to stuff a cushion for her mother. Taking out her paper and pencil Jade looked up at Ollie and asked what she should write.

Ollie began dictating what he wanted her to write, "Daddy! You must trust in us and not be afraid or tell others what we are doing. The seagull that gave our letter to you is called Philippe from France and he can talk to you. Our animal friends are going to help you escape and come home to us. Keep faith and expect a few surprises along the way. Lots of love from your daughter Jade." The next thing to do was to find a way to tie it around Samuel's body so that he could carry it back to Belgium and their father. Stretching his wing tips out and wriggling his tail feathers from side to side, Samuel raised off the ground saying, "Wish me luck" before disappearing up through the roof and heading off up into the sky.

Back across the sea in Belgium, Ken was preoccupied trying to understand the meaning of what he had been told the previous night and its meaning as well as to his own sanity. The harsh and loud bellowing out voice of the commanding German officer soon focused his attention back onto his situation and soon had him joining his comrades being marched in a column, like wild animals, along the road. Splashing through the many dirty, slushy puddles that kept popping up as he marched, Ken paid as much attention as he could to the surrounding area be it the landscape, the countless ruined buildings dotted with bullet marks or the burned out remains and even the bombed out shell of a church with its shattered stained glass windows.

They had been marching for about five hours without a drink or even a break for a rest when the bright flashes of explosions coupled with the deafening sound of battle to their left caused the soldiers guarding them to pause in the shelter of an orchard while deciding in which direction to proceed. After surviving the devastation of the Somme, Ken was thankful for the tree trunk that still grew there for him to rest against, shaded by the remaining leaves still on the branches. Somehow he found himself scouring the sky looking out for the sight of a seagull delivering him something to help although he had no idea of what it might be or even if the bird could find him, but as would soon happen he need not be worried.

It was four thirty pm when a dark spot appeared in the distance getting larger and recognizable as a seagull as it approached. This white and grey seagull, carrying something tied around its belly, was Samuel accompanied by Philippe, a little smaller than

Samuel but never the less still a welcome sight after only seeing rats clambering over the fallen bodies of his friends whilst fighting in the trenches. Both birds landed on a branch high up in the tree before, to the amazement of Ken, dropping down to stand at his feet. If this was not surprising enough already, Ken had the shock of his life, making him jump to his feet when Samuel spoke defying everything that he ever knew, "Quick! Take this letter off me. Untie it and don't ruffle my feathers. My friend Philippe will be helping you, trust him and for heaven sake don't eat him" then letting out a squawk lifted up into the sky flying away.

Once Samuel had left Ken unrolled the letter that he had been given from Jade his daughter. Recognizing her hand writing he became all choked up, trying to hold back the tears welling up inside him. He now knew that his own army was not the ones that were going to rescue him but his own lovely children aided by, believe it or not, animals and wild ones at that. He had no idea what to expect and was fearful for them, but he had always believed in and been proud of his little treasures, now he had to put his trust in them as well which was not a problem for him. Now it was Philippe's turn to come down from the branch to talk with Ken who was still looking at the letter blotted by his tears received from Jade. "We must get you away from the others by the time you reach the coast and find a way to hide you until help arrives." he explained before saying "I have to go to make plans now but I'll be back as soon as I can.". Just as Samuel had previously done Philippe flew off in the direction of the coast leaving Ken to think of what he would need to do now.

Philippe, knowing that there would be difficulty ahead in getting Kenneth away from the Hun, needed to check the route leading to the coast and identify any potential escape points, which he did finding one only an hour from the docks. Now he needed to arrange help from other animals, but which ones could he turn to. He firstly thought of the other birds then the mice, dogs and cats but when he heard the buzzing sound of Bernice the honey bee he knew. Getting her attention Philippe shared his mission and plan with her which she said, "Yes I will easily get help for you from the queen bee because the horrible Germans have destroyed our access to flowers to get the nectar for making honey with their bombs and burning everywhere. Many of my brothers and sisters have died because of them. I will be right back with her highness." It was 't to long before the queen bee wearing her crown with a yellow and black striped robe flanked by several guard bees' arrived with Bernice to make arrangements with Philippe. After almost an hour discussing the options that where open to them, they decided on what course of action to, take leaving Philippe to past it on to Ken.

It was the following morning, as Kenneth being marched by his captors, was feeling positive and confident saw out of the corner of his eye the approaching swarm of bee's and he knew exactly what he must do. Like a thick cloud of fog, the swarm engulfed the men surprisingly only covering the guards causing complete chaos, panic and terror for them. This action was the signal Kenneth waited for to take advantage of the confusion and run as fast as he could to the low stone wall bordering the road and jumping over it. Landing on the soft grass on the other side of the wall he rolled over and over before crawling behind a larger thicket of thorns before daring to stop.

"Bonjour you must be Kenneth. Get up onto my back and I'll take you somewhere safe." was an instruction from a horse named Albert, so up he got and off they ran across the battle scarred fields toward a fallen down building for shelter. As they galloped away Albert told of how he had been used by the French army to pull a wagon of supplies but was left behind after being attacked by the other side. Once in the clear Kenneth looked back across the field in time to see his new little bee friends dispersing to clear the air around his fellow prisoners and his guards trying to deal with the many stings that now covered them permitting him to chuckle at their predicament. As he much later related to his lovely wife if he had 't been right there, he surely would not have believed it possible. Sheltering inside the destroyed farm house until all of the enemy had moved on Kenneth asked his four legged savior, "What do I have to do now?" to which he was told that with his help they must find their way to an inlet just north of the port that he was being taken to.

` Bright and early the next morning Kenneth awoke to see his brown horse friend Albert standing powerfully by his side. "What do we do now?" asked Kenneth hoping for an encouraging answer while expecting to wake up and find himself still a prisoner. "For now we must hide from the enemy and make our way to where a boat will come for you and take you home." came the much welcomed news from Albert. While Kenneth hid within the remains of the farm house Albert went off to check on the preparations.

Finding his way across the fields whilst avoiding contact with any humans Albert found the easiest route for Kenneth to take to reach and cross the narrow canal that led to the coast. His spirits were raised immensely when he saw his friend circling overhead presumably looking for him. "Squawk squawk I 'm here my friend." cried out Philippe as he flew down to reach him. Very quickly Albert relayed what news he could from the last time they spoke about private Ingles escape from his captors and the bravery of the bees and of course his own gallant race to take him away from danger, exaggerating his own personal risk. "Good, now you have to keep him safe until Samuel can get a boat here for him." was the reply. "How long will that be?" asked Albert, to which he was told "Not long. I 'm off to see Samuel now." With that he lifted off into the warm cloudy sky again.

Back across the water in England things were being planned by Ollie and the rest. They had to find a way to get a boat across the channel to meet Kenneth and then get him back to his home shores. They had been scratching their heads for a while when Bernard the badger entered the barn with an idea that would carry some risk but could be done all the same. Taking the lead and with a deep, clear voice started sharing his proposal, "If we follow Carters brook to the river and then follow it down stream to the estuary we can borrow a boat to cross to the other side." "That's a great idea. When do we go?" asked Asa who had stopped playing on the tractor when Bernard had entered. All three children knew that this would be a big under taking but where determined to take it on because bringing their father home again was the most important thing to them. Now Ollie being concerned about the children emphasized the importance of not taking any serious risks, and told Samuel to find Sidney the seal as only he could contact Daisy the dolphin because they would need her help with the adventure ahead of them. Before setting off on their quest Ollie gave one more piece of advice, "Sidney can be trusted but he can also be very grumpy."

For the first time ever the three children found themselves walking a long distance without their parents or any other adult which was both nervy and exciting for them. For Kaya, the thought of being separated from her mother, was to a certain extent scary but being with her brother, sister and her new friends in the animal kingdom made everything easier whilst for Jade and Asa this was a chance to prove to the world that they could do anything. Getting to Carters brook the children accompanied by Bernard, Sammy and the field mice watched over by Ollie himself flying overhead, had to cross two fields and a farmers' mud track before climbing over a wooden fence and struggling through an over grown ditch before seeing the clear running water of the gently flowing brook.

Still being some distance from the sea the children were understandably getting more and more frustrated by the length of time that it was taking, but Ollie gave them a boost when he swooped down to them and directed them to a small rowing boat that could carry them down river. Standing on the river bank Jade surveyed the scene deciding on the best course of action for them all in relation to getting into the boat and more so getting it out into the water and moving it down stream. As luck would have it barely six feet away lay a piece of plank suitable for enabling Sammy and Bernard to board the boat. Bernard was very hesitant with the concept of leaving the stability of solid earth to walk up a narrow strip of wood over water but he was encouraged by everyone and by seeing Sammy bounding up that same plank gave him the courage needed. Sitting down on a lump of harder earth Jade carefully removed her shoes before hitching up her dress and wading into the water to push the boat free of the bank before climbing into it. Jade took her place at the front of the boat beside Bernard who had managed to lift himself up to peer over the rim while Asa and Kaya held their arms over the edge to paddle. It wasn't long until they were caught by the river current and were moving along quite steadily.

It was just as Carters Brook was joining onto the main river leading to the coast that everything became potentially disastrous for them. The boat was suddenly started to rock from side to side by the force of water leaving all of them clinging on for dear life. They were screaming out in panic as water splashed over the side and into the boat flooding it but worse was yet to come as a big wave swamped them washing Sammy over the edge and into the powerful current. Crying out to him, Asa was just about to dive into the river, when like a guardian angel Ollie swooped down with his claws open plucking Sammy up and carrying him to safety on the river bank. Now there was only Bernard to help them as

Ollie had to help Sammy back to the barn where he could get help from the other animals. Knowing their friend was still alive and safe the children's panic subsided allowing them to concentrate on reaching the coast and making contact with grumpy Sidney. Reaching the mouth of the river the boat was washed to the sandy beach by the gentle rippling waves of the English Channel.

Not going very far from the boat they didn't 't have too long to wait before the dark grey shape of a seal appeared coming up out of the water belly flopping its way toward them. "Samuel told me to leave what I was doing and come here. I'm here now. So what do you want?" grunted out Sidney in a grumpy voice, just as Ollie had warned them he would be like. Asa quickly joined in by telling him that their friend said that he would be able to get Daisy the dolphin to help them to cross over the sea to rescue their father. "I could, but it might take me a long time to find her and I will want payment for it. Let's say, five fresh fish." came Sidney's condition for doing what he had been asked. "If you do it quickly we'll get you ten fish." offered Kaya not really knowing how one earth they would manage to do it, but if it got daddy home again then they would find a way. "If you use the ebbing high tide to pull your boat out into the open sea I'll find Daisy and bring her to you" said Sidney flopping his way back into the water and disappearing under the waves.

They only had an hour and a half to wait until the high tide turned and began to flow back out pulling the little rowing boat carrying the three young child adventurers, along with Bernard the badger. The sun was beginning to set in the west when the dorsal fin of Daisy appeared breaking the surface of the water and revealing the white lace bonnet worn by her. She already knew the plan thanks to Samuel telling her all about it when he found her earlier that day. "OK, my dears you will need to tie a rope to the front of your boat and I will pull you as near as I can to where you need to be." said Daisy in a soft and reassuring voice. Looking down into the bottom of the boat, Asa found a long enough length of rope and tied it as well as he could to the anchor ring on the front before throwing the other end onto the sea for Daisy to take hold of with her mouth.

Meanwhile Kenneth riding on Albert's back had sneaked their way as close as they could without being discovered by the dastard German army. The most risky thing for Kenneth was crossing the canal in order to be on the correct side for when his rescuers arrived for him. Holding on tightly to him in the fading light Albert walked into the water and as it got deeper he started to doggy paddle toward the opposite side, but when they were only half way across shape of a craft appeared in the distance heading straight for them. "Oh no! They'll see the others and catch them" gasped Kenneth scared for his rescuers ignoring the fact that he was between them and the Germans. As luck would have it a sudden earth shattering explosion over to the south east which lit up the sky very quickly had the crew onboard focusing their attention on a far off point to where they were giving Albert sufficient time to reach the other side of the canal. It only took a couple of minutes to reach the relative safety of the bank where by ducking and diving to avoid being seen he managed to hide close to the water's edge. Both Kenneth and Albert were greatly thankful when the enemy war boat turned to move back the way it had come, and not only that but a small spec in the distance emerging out of the near darkness showing a small boat with three figures. His own young children accompanied by a wild badger.

"What are you three doing here?" cried out Kenneth as he waded out into the water toward the boat grabbing the edge of it pulling it back toward the bank. "Quick daddy, we have to leave here quickly before they see us." demanded Jade taking control of the situation. Carefully Kenneth clambered into the boat, trying extra hard not to rock it and tip it over. As Albert pushed them back out into the river flow, all onboard thanked him and wished him good luck in the future. As they floated back out into the sea leading to English shores and home all three children tried explaining to their father how they had come to be there and the magic spell they had made to make it happen. Any other person would normally dismiss all this as just children's wild tales but for Kenneth everything that he had experienced over the previous days told him to believe. This was helped when Daisy's fin appeared alongside them and her white bonneted head rose up out of the water to congratulate them on their escape. Before her taking hold of the rope which still dangled over the side.

After some hours of Daisy pulling the boat through the water the unmistakable shape of the English coastline appeared on the horizon having them all cheering with excitement at being nearly home. But before they could land they had to make a plan on explaining how Kenneth had escaped and got back home without any assistance from his superiors. "We can't tell anyone" demanded Kaya referring to the animals and what they could do. "You're right" said her father reassuringly "That must stay our secret kids, not even your mother can know our secret." They all sat silently for a few minutes trying to think of what to do when Bernard who had been laid down in the bottom of the boat came up with another good idea. Looking up at Kenneth he said, "Why don't you get out near the beach and we will go on ahead of you so the children can be at home when you get there." They all thought this a great idea and after thanking Daisy for her selfless help, Kenneth climbed over the edge of the boat and started swimming the last few yards to the sandy beach.

Now for the children they still had to make their way back to the barn and their friends before returning to their home and mother. It was getting dark again on another day when above them high in the sky the welcoming hooting of Ollie could be clearly be heard as they reached Carters Brook. "We did it!" shouted Asa triumphantly "Well done young man." came his response only for Kaya to add, "What about us, we were there to." "Very true you were all heroes'"came Ollie's reply. It wasn't't until the following morning just as the sun began shining through the thin clouds that the children spotted the old barn where a large number of animals had gathered to welcome them home. Even Samuel had come for this celebration but amid all of the joy there was still concern for Albert who was still trapped in the middle of a war, but their worries were soon eased by Philippe flying in with news that he had been rescued by a local farmer and was being cared for by him. Preparing to leave Asa suddenly remembered a promise he had made to Sidney the seal to get him ten fish for finding Daisy for them, but Ollie reassured him that he need not worry about it as Sidney gets all the fish he wants already.

Happy that everything was okay and as it should be again, the children departed heading for home and their mother, knowing that very soon their father would be getting back again where he belonged. As they walked back through the garden arch and saw their home a bright flash of light let them know that the adventure was over for now and to the world around them, no time had passed at all. What had been, for them almost a full week, was on the other side of the garden archway, had only been a few seconds. Nonetheless they had missed their mother immensely and rushed back into the house to see her.   Although they couldn't't tell of their adventure Gloria was undoubtedly suspicious of the sudden attention being paid to her by her children. For the rest of that day the children busied themselves making sure that they had left nothing out, not even dirty clothes, which had their mother even more suspicious as she was used to picking up things after them.

When Gloria entered the kitchen to find the busy children

cleaning it frantically she had to ask, "Okay you three, what are you up to. Have you broken something." expecting to hear a confession of some sort but what was to happen surprised even her. A knock at her front door distracted her attention causing her to about turn and leave the room again intending to return and get an account of the children's activity.

The caller at the door was none other than Mr. Pickering the local vicar, tall, skinny with receding grey hair and with a distinguished looking full beard. A man dreaded by wives of soldiers everywhere fearing bad news about their loved one. But on this day which was a Tuesday, the news couldn't't have been better. "Children come here; I have got something to tell you." Having a very good idea as to what it was, the children left what they were doing running out into the hallway to their mother who was clearly ecstatically happy. "My precious little treasures the vicar has just given me the best news in the whole world. Your daddy is coming home again." said Gloria with a massive smile on her face. After a short while and knowing what they had been busy doing all day, she looked directly at her children and asked "Did you lot know because it's very strange how you have been so helpful today?" "No mummy." was the reply from three smiling children as they rushed up to their mother. It was the following day after lunch that Kenneth returned home retaking his place as man of the house back. Everything was just as it should be again plus the big secret of Kenneth and his children still held firm but ended their wondrous adventures, but first there was something important for Kenneth to do. He wanted to go and see Ollie and the other animals to thank them for their help in rescuing him.

Using the excuse of showing Kenneth where they played and the den they made in the wooded area, the children took their father for a walk down over the garden toward the magical archway. Taking a hold of his hand Jade looked at her father and said," You have to keep a hold of my hand when we go through the archway or you won't be able to talk to the animals." so taking a firm hold they stepped under the arch. Just as happened with the children there was a bright flash of brilliant light with a tingling sensation all over them followed by nothing? The magical spell had worked on Kenneth and they were into a wondrous world. Intrigued by the experience passing through the archway Kenneth asked Jade if anybody could do as he had just done to which she told him that they couldn't because it was only her and her brother and sister who had done the spell. "You have to be careful where you step now daddy so you don't squash any small animals." instructed Kaya. "Sammy!" Called out Asa as they paused briefly to enable their father to observe the surroundings, calling again, "Bernie, Dora where are you?"

Kenneth was astounded when from out of a clump of thistle appeared Sammy wearing his bright red– pull over carrying a rolled up newspaper to take to Ollie. "Where did you get that from?" enquired Jade inquisitively. "Oh err I get it from the vicarage before it is thrown away." admitted Sammy a bit hesitantly "Ollie likes to keep informed about humans. All I have to do is avoid the horrible cat that lives there.". "That's amazing" said Kenneth flabbergasted by what he was seeing and hearing before him. Kaya on hearing this straight away salid, "Daddy can we get the paper for Ollie because we don't have any cats or dogs to catch Sammy. Please daddy." Okay Kaya we can do that and I'll put you in charge of it." This pleased her very much as it gave her the feeling of importance and responsibility. Sammy was also thankful as it meant that she wouldn't have to face that terrible cat called Spatey. With that sorted Kenneth requested they carry on and visit Ollie as he carried the rolled up newspaper for him.

As they continued to walk toward the old barn Kenneth was taking as much notice as he could while asking many questions about the animals that were able to talk to them and of course about the spell that the children had used to make all this possible. After climbing over the old rotting wooden gate into the field where the barn was Asa rushed off ahead as Kenneth and the girls strolled leisurely along behind. Reaching the barn door they were greeted by the field mice and accompanied by them as they entered. "This is our friend Ollie." proclaimed Asa directing his hand up the wall and pointing at him.

"I am very happy to meet and thank you for arranging my escape and rescue. I will try to do anything I can to show you just how much your help meant to Me." said Kenneth looking up at Ollie who had come out of his dark notch high in the wall. "Thanks are not necessary sir, your children are good friends to all the animals and while you were away they were sad so we had to help do something. Oh good. Is that the newspaper I see in your hand?" asked Ollie. "It sure is. I 'm carrying it for Sammy." was his reply as he passed it back to climb up the wall to give him. For the next two hours they all sat around talking getting to know each other better.

As they talked the subject of Bernice the bee and her difficult finding any flowers or blossom to make honey came up which worried Kenneth remembering the incredible action all the bees carried out to help him to escape. "If only they were here because we would let them use our garden and its plants to make as much honey as they wanted." stated Kenneth which immediately got Ollie thinking of ways that could make that so, With that the children and father departed to return home again to Gloria and their afternoon cup of tea and slice of cake.

It wasn 't until several days later that whilst placing the finished with newspaper where they had arranged for Sammy to get it from that Kaya noticed him on the house side of the archway trying to attract her attention. Because on this side neither were able to talk and the animals looked no different to how anybody else saw them other means of communicating had to be used. Sensing something important she dashed to the archway and stepping through closely by Sammy eager to pass on the news. "Ollie says can you bring your father to see him tomorrow about Bernice and what can be done to help." Sure enough she would tell her daddy as soon as she could and would see him the next day.

The following day after they had finished their lunch Kenneth took the children out for a walk taking advantage of the warm and sunny day making their way directly for the barn and Ollie's news. "Claudette the queen of the bees has decided that they are going to come here to stay here in the barn and thanks you very much for your offer to use your garden to gather nectar for honey." informed Ollie making Kenneth thankful for the opportunity to help and repay their earlier assistance in his rescue. With Kaya already having the job of having the newspaper ready for Sammy, the job of keeping the garden watered fell to Asa while Jade's job would be plucking off dead flowers and pulling up troublesome weeds. On his part Kenneth offered to construct small shelters for the bees to use.

It was only three days later that a flock of seagulls landed near the barn carrying the dozens of bees on their backs protected by the feathers of the birds. The sight of a garden full of blooming flowers greatly pleased queen Claudette causing her to promise to make some honey especially for Kenneth's family as a thank you for their kindness. Once again by helping and working together humans and animals had solved and overcome a difficulty. For the rest of the summer and autumn life was great for the children and their parents bringing them even closer than before but as all things must come to an end as for most of the animals it was time to hibernate and go to sleep until the spring. Then on one day during the month of November there was no bright flash or tingling sensation as they passed through the garden arch. Was the magic over for them? Not

Even reciting the spell worked for them.

Adventure Two Saving Bernie

The Great War was nearing an end and all was calm and relaxed with Kenneth Ingle's fighting days over with. Even our three young adventurers had nothing to concern themselves with two years after his rescue from the Hun. It was a Sunday afternoon toward the end of April in 1918 that the three who were lazing around on the grassed back garden of their family home, when an old friend attracted their attention from beyond the other side of the archway that led to the wooded area at the end of the garden. "Whose that." asked Kaya really recognizing a voice that she knew all too well as a friend in deed, At the time she was in the process of dressing the doll given to her as a Christmas present by her grandparents during a family get together. "It's me, Sammy your friend in the woods." came his reply, perking the attention of all three children. "How is that possible? The spell that lets us talk with you was broken after we rescued daddy two years ago." enquired Jade who had raised herself on to her elbows from the ground to see what was going on. "Ollie needs to speak with all of you. We need your help." Being inquisitive as all children tend to be at their age the trio jumped to their feet and rushed across the lawn to the archway at the end of it. Peering through the gap Asa was the first to see on the ground before them, their friendly squirrel Sammy wearing a knitted red polo neck jumper with his bushy tail coming out from it.

Not understanding why after so long of not being able to hear or see the animals, Jade was the first to step through the archway closely followed by the other two. Every time that they had used it during the previous two years there had not been any response by passing through it but this time there was. A flash of bright light with a crackling sound greeted their entry into the magical world where animals could and had many times talked with them. For the children all this was a sure sign that they must be needed in some way, but for Kaya it felt as if she was only wanted when the animals wanted them for something. "Good, I'm so glad you've come." screeched Sammy relieved at the children's willingness to at least join him. Although both Jade and Asa were in a hurry to see their owl friend Ollie again Kaya dragged her feet not being in any kind of a hurry to find out what was required of them.

Entering the foot path that led to the small field housing Ollie the owl in his old stone barn, the two girls had to walk carefully owing to the earth track being considerably wet and muddy due to a heavy shower of rain earlier that morning. "Yuk" grumbled Kaya as her foot caught a particularly mucky bit leaving her foot indentation which soon filled with water, giving the others a reason to giggle." Stop laughing at me, or I am going home again." came her angry response even though she wanted to see Ollie again just as much as the others did. It was not too long before they were at the barn ready to find out for what reason they were wanted.

Standing on the ground below Ollie's favourite ledge Jade announced their arrival saying, "We are here Ollie. Have you got a problem that we can help you with?". "To wit to woo Yes I'm very glad that you have come my friends. We need your help as never before." came his distressed plea. "Tell us all about it." instructed Jade as she sat herself down on an old wooden crate. Seeming to clear his throat Ollie began to reveal the trouble shared by all of the animals in the direct area. "Sprinter the fox who lives in the next valley has let us know that Mr. Simpson who owns all of the land around here is selling it to build a factory where my home is, and other animals too." pausing before continuing with, "We need your help if we are going to save our homes from being buried under concrete and tarmac forever. Even your home will be pulled down." This news greatly upset all of the children. "I won't let them take our home away, not ever!" swore Asa angrily "He's right, we'll find a way to beat them." came Jade's agreement with her brother. "Maybe daddy can help." added Kaya still trying to scrape the muck off her shoes picked up while getting there. With that said the children returned home again back along the muddy footpath and through the magic archway that only they and their father could do.

Back at home the children were being mysteriously quite for a change which caught their parent's attention and causing some suspicion by them. Kenneth who was now working as an assistant manager of a law firm concerned with property selling. Suspecting something was up Kenneth became inquisitive and when he was saying good night to the children he carefully chooses the right time and took Jade to one side, as they began climbing the narrow squeaky wooden staircase toward their bedrooms and asked her what was causing her obvious concern. "I don't know how to tell you daddy." said Jade trying to hold back from revealing how they had found that the magic spell was working again. Trusting herself not to do anything foolish without at least talking to him first about it.

All of that night Jade tossed and turned in her bed trying to decide on the best course of action to take over the problems concerning her family and all of her the animal friends. Come the following day a Monday and a school day all three children couldn't wait until they returned home again so that they could go and see Sammy and the others. After leaving their school house and beginning the short walk up along the narrow country road that led home, and passed the poorer children whose families could not afford schooling for their children. All three talked about the animal's predicament and wondered if by any chance there were any other children that could help them. "I know. We'll go and ask Ollie later." suggested Asa thinking he had thought of a good idea which was agreed with by his sisters. Before they could do anything they had to change out of their school clothing which for the girls consisted of a grey full length gown tied around the waist with a peace of rope and for Asa he had on his cleaned breaches and smart blazer.

Once changed into more suitable attire they had to have something to eat before going back into the wooded area where their animal friends lived. Just as the trio was about to go out of the rear door Kenneth entered the front door in an anxious mood causing them to pause in their tracks. "What worries you my husband?" asked Gloria his wife and children's mother showing concern for him, but trying hard to disguise his concern said, "Oh nothing my sweet I just had a difficult client to deal with." Turning to face the children he asked, "How would you three like to have your own tree house built in that big oak tree where you play." giving them a wink. "Oh yes please daddy." was the reply from his children. The children went outside to await their father as he prepared to join them in the wooded area outside of their garden.

Joining his children Kenneth guided them around the side of their house to the front entrance, and calmly strolled along the road toward a grown over wooden gate across the entrance to the mud track that led through the wooded area that the children played in. Seeing a wooden for sale sign sticking up out of the ground beside the gate Kaya insisted that her father take it down, but he explained that if he did that he might end up in serious trouble and to give him time to find a way to prevent it from being sold. "We'll do anything we can to help you daddy." said Jade trying to keep her obvious annoyance under control in front of her siblings. "I know that I can rely on you three not to do anything naughty." came his proud response. "Now, so your mother doesn't think that you're up to something I had better get back and you three had better go off and play or whatever." suggested Kenneth. With him returned to the house and Gloria who was sitting in the parlour stitching a hole in the leg of Asa's school trousers, the three children headed off through the archway, their destination being the old barn to see Ollie the owl and any of their other animal friends that might be there.

They had only just reached the barns side door when out of the corner of his eye Asa spied the sight of a dog like shape moving hurriedly in their direction. As it drew closer to them they were amazed to find sitting steadily on its back was none other than Sammy. As the two characters rushed through the door that Kaya had just pushed opened for them, "To wit to woo" could be heard coming from Ollie who had just emerged into the open from his dark corner high up in the wall. "Why are you rushing around in the open where you can be seen?" he asked aggressively. "It's that evil cat Spatey. She has cornered Bernie and is threatening to bite his head off and eat him if she can catch him." panted out Sprinter as he steadily raised himself up onto his back legs just as if he were human, Totally astonished at this sight Asa yelled out "Wow that's fantastic who taught him to do that trick?" "No trick there, Merlin made it so long ago." He paused a second before continuing with. "We have to stop her." pleaded Sammy grabbing at the hem of his red polo neck, to which all three children came out with," We'll stop her. Bernie is our friend.". "How can we help you?" came the low buzzing voice of Queen bee Claudette who had been disturbed from her sleep by all of the commotion. "Good." declared Ollie impressed at how they all wanted to help a friend in danger.

"Right. Here's what we shall do.". Looking down to his right toward Claudette Ollie began giving out his instructions. "Your majesty if you can you get some of your soldier bees to fly over to the vicarage and start pestering Spatey to stop her getting to Bernie before help can arrive," With that she popped back into the shelter that Kenneth had built for the bees, and after some buzzing out flew a group of bees of about twenty on a mission. That was the first step set in motion now for step two. "Sprinter and Sammy. You can easily outwit that horrible fat cat and most certainly out run her, so I want you two to steal her attention away from Bernie long enough for the children to pluck him away to safety. Finally turning his attention on to Jade said, "Well young lady. Are you up for a little good against bad action?" "Oh yes!" came the resounding answer from the trio as they turned and headed back out of the barn, destination the vicarage and the task set for them.

     `Meanwhile almost a mile away hiding in a small hole at the base of a concrete statue of a holy nun holding a prayer book, was Bernie trembling in fear of the wicked fat cat Spatey who was squatting down poised ready to pounce and gobble him up. Just as he was resigning himself to never seeing his loving wife Dora again, from out of the sky came the buzzing sound of bees swarming down at Spatey. One of the bees let herself known to Bernie as his friend Bernice her bee pals were going to keep the cat occupied until help arrived. You can't imagine the relieve on Bernie's little face at the help or even the joy he felt when Bernice flew straight at Spatey stinging her on the end of the nose causing her to cry out. Whilst Spatey was being kept occupied by Queen Claudette and her swarm of bees, Bernie was thankfully able to relax his fears of being eaten by the wicked cat.

Rushing just as fast as they could Sprinter with Sammy clinging tightly on to his back, hurried across the fields leaping a drainage ditch with a couple of inches of water in and climbing through hedges to reach their brave little friend in time to save him. "Slow down!" yelled out Sammy trying desperately to hold on as Sprinter ran down the sloping hillside that was at the rear of the vicarage. "Almost there my friend." barked Sprinter as he jumped a low wall obstacle gaining access to the vicarage garden. Straight away they could see the bees massing around Spatey driving her crazy and keeping her from getting to Bernie. Now it was their turn to have a go. Firstly, Sammy slid himself off from Sprinters back and waited for his friend to place himself in position ready for action.

Because they were not able to use the same route as the animals to get there, all three children were puffing and panting by the time they reached the vicarage, but they were all determined to save their friend from the wicked fat cat and take him home to his loving wife Dora. "Quickly Asa, we've got to get there on time." called back jade to her little brother who was lagging behind due to him being younger and smaller. "I'm going as fast as I can but you're bigger than I Am." was his reply at being shouted at for being slower. They really need not to panic too much about getting there to fast as Sprinter and Sammy were about to spring into action. With her part in Bernie's rescue complete Queen Claudette signaled to her bees to withdraw and pass over to the others.

As Sprinter hid amongst Mr. Pickering's vegetable patch Sammy moved not to close but close enough to attract Spatey's attention. As the bees departed Spatey turned her focus back on to getting Bernie, but Sammy got her gaze back and on to him. "I see you, you pesky little rodent. I'm going to get you." she said turning in his direction and moving toward him with a sluggish effort. Sammy seeing her coming darted off to about a dozen feet in front of her before turning to say," Hey fat cat. Bet you can't catch me.". This was what Sprinter was anxiously waiting for and his signal to move. Springing out of his hiding place amongst the Brussel sprout plants Sprinter ran hurriedly toward Spatey giving her a scare bad enough to make her forget all about Bernie and run as fast as she could to escape from her chaser, back through the house cat flap installed by the vicar for her. "Don't let me see you after any more of my friends again or I'll be back!", demanded Sprinter through the cat flap at Spatey who was hiding very frightened under a hallway stand.

"Are we in time?" panted Jade as the children came hurrying up the gravel path that led around the side of the vicarage to where our animal friends were. "You made it. He's safe now." smugly proclaimed Sammy trying to reassure Bernie into coming out of his hiding place. Hesitantly he emerged cheering up immensely at the sight of the children there. "Come along our friend. We'll take you home to Dora now she must be very worried." said Kaya very gently picking him up before saying bye to Sprinter and Sammy who turned to return to the barn to fill Ollie in on what had transpired with them.

Adventure Three Castle Hope

Stepping back through the archway into the world without talking animals the children were greeted by the sight of a short tubby business looking man making notes on a clipboard. Mr. Brown as they discovered he was called was discussing Mr. Simpson's plans for the wooded area and small field that housed the barn with their father. "Well it's like this." began Mr. brown as be started to explain to Kenneth the intended plan of Mr. Simpson the land owner. "He has decided to sell off a chunk of his land to a business company so it can build a new factory in the field with a new road giving access through the wooded area at the end of your rear garden which may involve your having to relocate because your home may need pulling down.".

"No! You can't do it." angrily shouted out Jade on over hearing what had just transpired. "What can we do about it?" asked Kenneth, "My children have never been as happy as they are here which goes for my wife and I also." Thinking hard about the situation Mr. Brown could only suggest either finding the necessary funds to purchase the land or finding Mrs. West the previous owner of the house and checking the estate deeds and ownership. A good idea thought Kenneth as he said goodbye to Mr. Brown thinking of the options open to him and his family. "Well my young princess, it's time for us to find Mrs. west wherever she may be and have a good talk with her."

The next few days saw Kaya and Asa checking every book that was stored in the crates in their attic from when Mrs. West had lived there, while Jade accompanied her father firstly to the records office in Newton Priory before talking to the vicar and local people about her. All in all, there was nothing on official record as to the location of her and it was a mystery to the locals as to where she had gone to. As a last resort Jade suggested talking to Ollie to find out if the animals had any ideas about her. So at the first opportunity they the children entered the world of the talking animals and made their way along the mud track way that led to the field which housed the barn where Ollie the owl lived.

`"To wit to woo, oh I remember her." said Ollie in answer to Jades question about Mrs. West. "She is a good lady. She used to be a friend to us all and has helped many times with injuries and the like before she got sick and set off to find some special medicine to get better again." "But where is she now?" enquired Kaya hoping for positive news. "Think it will be a waste of your time if I tell you because they don't exist out of legend." he very quickly responded. "Who doesn't exist?" She asked becoming quite intrigued by talk of legends. "The little people who can fly who are said live at Castle Hope many miles away." "Then that is where we must go" declared Jade determined to go wherever they must to find Mrs. West. "If you must go, I guess that Sprinter and maybe Sammy should join you in your quest." It was not long before plans were set in motion for the impending exhibition to find the mysterious little people and Mrs. West.

Bright and early two days later the children set off on their quest. Jade was wearing a shin length dress and a white cotton blouse with a frilled full collar looking quite a young lady while her younger sister Kaya was wearing a grey full length dress, and Asa was wearing a blue and brown checked cotton shirt with a pair of breeches and they were all wearing sturdy footwear. As they passed under the magical archway they were met by Bernie who expressed his regret at not being able to join them on their journey due to his having to stay behind for Dora and their four new babies. "Can I see them?" asked Kaya briefly distracted from the impending journey ahead of them. "I'm sorry my friend, you won't be able to see them yet but you will when you get back."

came his reply. So fueled with this information to look forward, to the three of them set off on their intended journey with no idea what to expect ahead of them.

Before going to far Jade suggested that they saw their friend Ollie for any advice on what to do. On reaching the old barn the children were met by Sammy who informed them that Ollie had already left because he had to visit his uncle who lived not too far from the ruins of Castle Hope, but he had been given directions for getting there. "Okay. So how do we get there?" asked Asa impatiently? "First you will have to wait for Sprinter to get here because we will need his help along the way. He's on his way to you already." Buzzed Queen Claudette who was just flying back into the hive that Kenneth had built them for helping him to escape and return home again during the war. They were soon joined by Sprinter and after having a quiet chat with Sammy they were setting off in the direction of Carters Brook.

"The last time that we came this way it was to go to the coast to rescue daddy." Jade reminded them of before enquiring why they were going that way again. "Yes, you are perfectly correct." said Sprinter, "But this time we must travel upstream for a whole day before crossing the open fields and rocky moor land. Are you sure that you are up to it?". "We have to be." answered Jade knowing that finding Mrs. West was vital to saving their home from being demolished. So with Sammy comfortably sat on Sprinters back the children began their long journey.

As they set off they were apprehensive as to what lay ahead of them, but Asa eased their worries by talking about how they were like explorers going into an unknown world. Having read several storybooks about fairy's, Kaya couldn't help but ask if that was what the mysterious little people were because Ollie had mentioned that they were supposed to fly to Sprinter, "But it will be magical if they are. According to legend they were just like you before but Merlin cast a spell to hide them from invaders that would of killed them all if he hadn't. It is said that he couldn't find them again when it was safe to take the spell off." "Well, let's just hope that they exist and we can find them." added Jade who was listening to what was said.

Having had travelled this way once before it didn't feel like to long before the clear sparkling water of Carters Brook could be seen glistening through the trees along its bank. "There's the Brooke announced Asa." happy that they had reached it. "Can we stop for something to eat now before we go on?" asked Kaya rubbing her belly. "Not yet, we still have a long way to go." answered jade "We only have the few sandwiches that I was able to sneak out when we left home." "If you want to there is a suitable spot where you can stop before we turn away from the Brooke to cross the fields and rough ground." said Sprinter. With Sprinter and Sammy leading the way, the children carefully followed along beside the Brooke, avoiding the overhanging tree branches and the sometimes thick nettles and thistles until they reached a clear entrance to a field that they had to cross.

About half way along the edge of the field stood a small lean—to shelter where Sprinter mindful of the coming night suggested they slept until the morning which was agreed on. Eating a sandwich of homemade strawberry jam each as they prepared to settle down for the night the children talked about the following day and what it entailed. They talked for some time guessing as to what they had to do before Sprinter spoke. "In the morning you can use the water trough outside to have a quick wash and then we have to cross several more fields until we meet an old track way that will lead us to the higher rough ground not far from the castle ruins where the little people are said to live, so get yourselves to sleep now while we watch over you.". Turning to Sammy he gave an instruction to take the first watch and he would take over after four hours.

Bright and early the next morning just as the many wild birds were beginning to sing their dawn chorus, Sprinter woke the children and Sammy, "Wake up you lot. We need to get going soon." Within the hour all three children had managed to brave the cold water to wash their faces and eat another sandwich ready to go. The day was warmish but a light breeze had the scattered clouds moving swiftly across the sky frequently covering the sun, but at least it was dry which was lucky as the children had brought no water proofs with them. The five of them crossed over three fields by midday and then reached a gate that opened onto what Sprinter identified as the old track way that they must follow to the castle. As they travelled along the track they noticed the Ash and Sycamore trees that lined it slowly becoming spread wider apart until there were no more trees and only rough scrub remained. They had reached the base of the higher ground surrounding the castle ruins that could now be seen standing prominently on the horizon.

"Wow! Is that where the little people are?" gasped Kaya on seeing the size of the ruins. "I bet it's full of skeletons and ghosts and there may be a dragon in the dungeon." Commented Asa as he started running up the sloping path toward the fallen down entranceway full of excitement at what they would find. They were barely a dozen feet away from their goal when out of the sky above them came a sound that they all instantly recognized, "To wit to woo" it was Ollie swooping down toward them. Beckoning them to come to him Ollie landed on top of a large stone that was once part of the castles battlements. "Gather around, I have much to tell you before you enter here." The five intrepid adventurers gathered before him eager to hear whatever news Ollie had for them.

With them all gathered and paying attention Ollie outstretched his wings before continuing with, "Once you are inside the ruins look for an engraving of a hawk standing on top of a skull. When you find it let me know so I can give you instructions on what you must do, but be very careful because the whole place could fall down on to you, and that would never do.." Not even Kaya who was normally very cautious and safety minded hesitated before climbing the moss covered stone steps toward what used to be a solid oak doorway to the great hall. As it was there was only the four crumbling walls of what had once been a two story building and must in its day have been a magnificent center of power and control for the surrounding land. Pushing the smaller rubble to the side with their feet as they stepped through the doorway all eyes were scouring in every direction looking for a hawk. Sammy being smaller and more agile was able to get to areas that were not accessible to the larger children often coming back covered with dust and a few spiders' webs. After several hours of searching with no luck they were heartened by Sprinter as he was reversing back out from under a pile of fallen masonry yelling, "I've found it. It's been buried under all this rubble. We had better go tell Ollie what we found. He can tell us what to do now." So turning toward the doorway the five rushed back out to tell Ollie of their discovery and ask him what they should do now.

"Well my young friends, it appears that you have a hard job ahead of you to clear enough space to reach the engraving but first, Sprinter could you see any indentations where the eyes are?" said Ollie making sure that he had indeed found the right engraving. "It must be the right one. The eyes looked like deep holes." replied Sprinter feeling quite pleased with himself for noticing. Being aware of

Asa's younger age Ollie decided to give him the task of finding anything that his sisters could use to pry any stones away if needed, and then to Jade and Kaya he told them to only clear away what they needed to. With instructions given the children once again headed back into the ruins to start clearing a way through to the engraving. Asa wandered off to find anything to help and to do a bit of exploring for himself.

He looked around what was once a great hall with his eyes moving along each wall and taking note of any potential areas to look closer at. Built into the wall at the far end opposite the entrance doorway Asa spied the large fireplace that would of supplied heat for the people that once lived there and ruled the land. As his gaze moved along the wall he noticed a veil of ivy hanging down in the corner to his right from where he could feel a breeze coming from behind. Curiosity soon found him pulling at the ivy to find what was hidden behind it. His excitement was soon given a boost by the discovery of the bottom half dozen winding stone steps that once led up to an upper floor. He carefully went up as far as he was able to being aware of the many smaller stones that had fallen over the years from further up. Meanwhile back in the grand hall Jade and Kaya had moved as much rubble as they could but there were still several chunks of masonry that were preventing them from proceeding due to their size and weight. It was looking as if all the girls hard work had been wasted but Sammy who had come in to warn them that it was starting to get dark, so they should all return outside to camp until morning and they might find a way tomorrow. Jade looked up to see the moon starting to show through the space that was once covered by another floor and a roof before taking one last attempt at moving one large jagged piece of masonry before joining to the others who were ready to go.

Getting back outside Sammy directed them to a smaller piece of standing wall about six feet high where Ollie and Sprinter were waiting for them. "We could not do it, it's all too big and heavy for us." sobbed Jade wiping a small tear from her eye clearly upset at the situation. "Never mind young lady. Nobody could ask from more of you great children. In the morning I will fly over to my Uncle to see if he can suggest anything." proudly said Ollie before adding, "Oh I have managed to bring you a blanket to wrap yourselves in." but by this time they were to tired to explain how he had brought it or where from. With the sun going down behind the horizon the children laid them down sheltered by the wall behind them, and looked up at the sparkling stars in a cloudless night sky before falling asleep. It was about two o'clock in the morning that they were awakened by the loud crashing sound of something heavy moving inside the ruins. Fearing the worst Ollie decided that they should do nothing until the morning.

The arrival of the morning was to prove to be the start of a series of what the children could only call magical happenings. The first of these happenings came when Asa went up to the doorway and peered in not knowing what to expect. Spinning around Asa in astonishment at what he saw shouted to the others, "Quick! You have to see this." The girls who were still in the process of sorting themselves out ready for the new day left what they were doing to go to their brother and find out what had got him so worked up. As they reached the first step leading up to Asa Jade asked, "What are you so excited about?" before looking in and seeing for herself. Kaya, Sprinter and Sammy soon joined them in the doorway looking in speechless and open mouthed by what they saw.

All of the heavy rubble that the girls could not move the previous day had mysteriously gone leaving a clear pathway to the engraving. Not only that but also laid out on top of the grass that covered the floor was three goblets full of fresh milk straight from the cow, a plate with sandwiches, several hard boiled eggs, and a bowl with fresh apples, plums and strawberries in. Licking her lips Kaya headed straight for the food picking up a sandwich and taking a big bite before enquiring as to where it had all come from. "It's obviously meant for us, there is only three drinks." said Asa, picking up a goblet and taking a drink out of it giving himself a milk moustache in the process. The way that all these things just appeared over night was very mysterious and magical to the children.

After having something to eat Jade suggested going back outside to ask Ollie what they should do now and if he had any idea who was responsible for helping them. "I do not know but I do have a couple ideas of who." said Ollie not really wanting to put him on the spot. "Go on tell us. We won't get angry if you're wrong." pleaded Jade. "Okay, okay I'll tell you. It is possible that either the little people are real and in some way have the power to move heavy things, or Mrs. West is around and can do those things. I am almost certainly wrong but I have no other explanation to offer." said Ollie hesitantly. "That's what I was thinking." replied Jade trying to make her friend feel better. "If it was the little people, where are they and how do we see them?" added Kaya. "If it was them we will only see them if they want you to." said Ollie not wanting to build her hopes up.

With that all over Jade asked why they had needed to find and clear a way to the engraving of a hawk inside the hall. "From what I understand about it you will need to poke your fingers into the eye sockets to trigger a mechanism, to open a hidden door that allows you to get to where the little people are thought to exist." explained Ollie. So without any delay the children led by Kaya eager to see if the little people were fairy's or just little people, rushed back into the great hall to where the engraving was. Stepping up onto the large stone block that had been left below the hawk to reach, Jade carefully pushed her fingers into the eye sockets causing a deep sounding cranking noise as if a heavy door was trying to open, but they could see nothing happening. "I guess that after hundreds of years being empty and falling down it is broken now." said Sammy in a sympathetic voice. "Maybe it just needs oiling." said Asa but they were all clearly disappointed by this until Kaya reminded them of what had happened the night before. "Why don't we go out and tell Ollie to see what he thinks we can do now." suggested Jade. So they all turned and moved toward the doorway heading back outside, but something caught Kaya's eye. Could it be, had she just caught a glimpse of one of the little people? Before she had the chance to say anything it seemed to disappear again so she carried on going outside with the others.

Now back outside of the ruins again the children sat themselves down on top of a few scattered fragments of broken wall with Ollie to discuss the whole situation and what could be done now. Kaya relayed what she thought she saw when leaving which had Ollie scratching his beak with the tip of one of his wings deep in thought. After considerable time thinking about this Ollie finally had to admit to being stumped for an idea, but Jade decided that she was going to stay right there until the little people revealed themselves to her. With thoughts of home and images of it being knocked down in her mind she told her sister and brother that they could return home again if they wanted but she was staying until the little people talked to her. In a very harsh tone Asa said, "No way. We are not going to leave you now. We'll stay at your side no matter how long for." With that the three children followed by the animals once again returned into the remains finding a comfortable place to sit for their vigil. It was after midnight that a sound of something small scurrying around could be made out in the dark which the children knew was not Sprinter or Sammy as they were curled up asleep next to them. Sitting up straight Jade spoke out, "I know you are there watching us. Please talk with me; we need your help to find Mrs. West so we can save ours and the animal homes from being destroyed. We will never tell of you to anyone unless you say so." Everything went quiet straight after she had finished speaking and she feared that she had frightened them away, but she hadn't as they were all about to discover come the following morning.

Adventure Four Finding Mrs. West

The next day after a night of taking turns to be awake watching and listening for any sign of the little people, the tiny figure of a man about six inches in height with long flaming red hair appeared standing on a stone about two feet in front of them. Pandar as they found out he was called was dressed in green animal skin leggings, wearing moccasin boots and a waist coat but nothing else except for a bow hung over his shoulder said, "Why are you looking for Mrs. West and how do you know about us?" to which Jade told of everything they knew and why they were there. "Wait here while I tell our King and get his orders." Where his reply from Pandar before he jumped down from where he was and disappeared into a large area of vegetation below him and going off. With him out of sight Kaya was able to express her disappointment at him not having wings like she hoped for.

Nearly three hours later four mice wearing miniature saddles with riders on appeared from the side of what was a long time before been a big fireplace. The riders were all dressed the same as Pandar but carrying a spear fashioned out of the spine of a hedgehog. "Oh wow! Gasped Kaya." astonished by what she was witnessing before her. "I wish Ollie could see this." said Jade, "Is that Ollie the owl? I've heard the stories about him from Lizzy. Oops I mean Mrs. West." raised a voice from nearby. It was Pandar climbing up onto the same place as he was earlier that day. "Yes, he is our friend and he helped us rescue our daddy.". "Oh", was an astonished gasp before continuing, "That must be Kenneth who must make you Jade, Kaya and Asa, his children. We know all about you." "You know who we are, that's fantastic." said Asa feeling very important. Sammy added, "Why don't I pop out and get Ollie so you can all talk?"

It only took a few minutes before through the space where a roof once was flew Ollie gracefully gliding down to the ground ensuring he did not land on anybody. "I am very pleased to meet you." said Ollie clearly happy with the choices and ideas which he had had up until to then. Looking for confirmation Ollie said to Pandar," I presume that you have been told the reason why these children have travelled so far from their home and parents to seek you out." "Yes they have. Our king wants to meet with them to talk of this before he makes a decision on whether to help in your difficult situation. "Thank you very much. Let's go and see him now" said Jade in eagerness. With that Pandar instructed Jade on what she must do, "Right we already know you have tried to open the door to our domain, now you have to finish opening it by putting your fingers into the mouth of the skull." With that Kaya hurried over to the engraving pausing briefly for a second or two before hesitantly pushing her index finger into the mouth part of the skull sending a nervy shiver through her whole body. As Jade and Asa reached their sister the rough scraping sound of stone grinding against stone came from the inside wall of the large fire place coupled with a small puff of dust. That was it; they had found and opened the secret door to find the mysterious little people.

Staying close the children led by Pandar on foot and a few of his warriors, were guided through the doorway filled with trepidation over what they were about to encounter. A long narrow damp and dirty passageway with small drops of water dripping onto the ground only added to their anxiety, but they knew that if they were going to save their home they had to carry on. Their worries were only added to when Pandar announced that the children would have to be shrunk to his height to continue any further. As for the others unfortunately Sprinter and Ollie were not permitted to follow them into where they now were, but Sammy being a lot smaller was and he was a great giver of encouragement as they went along. They had only travelled a short distance when they approached a sharp corner where light could be seen coming from. Going around the corner the children saw for the first time in hundreds of years the inside of what had been the dudgeon of a Norman castle. They were in an area outside of the cells where prisoners were kept. Asa was very intrigued at this and couldn't wait to find out who or what was still in the cells. So he went straight for the nearest cell to him and peered intuitively through the rusty bars not really knowing what he would see. Jade was more interested in why it was so light there when they were under the ground. Pandar who was down by her side said, "Merlin cast a spell on the walls to make them shine out in the dark so that we can see clearly." "Oh wow that's fantastic." shouted Asa as he saw hanging from the wall an iron cage containing a skeleton. This frightened Kaya somewhat but none the less it did not cause her to want to leave. Not even the skulls, rusty swords and dented armor that were scattered around on the floor could sway them from the purpose of their mission. So forward they continued until Pandar told them to stop where they were. They had reached the entrance to the secret realm of the little people where only one person from their land had ever been. To continue this was where they had to be shrunk to his size so without hesitation all three prepared for this.

A cloud of powder blown over them was all it took to see the roof of the tunnel moving upward away from them as they became small enough to be the same height as Pandar. For the first time the girls showed some regret at this when they saw what was previously a small harmless spider dropping down from above now looking so much bigger and scarier, A small door only about two feet high and made out of a solid single piece of oak was all that stood between the children and the help they needed for themselves and their animal friends. They had no idea of what to expect on opening it but Jade took a deep breath and went in, closely followed by her Sister and Brother.

Passing through the door the children were astounded by what they saw. It was just as if they had left the ruins and before them they found fields, trees and even a river all under a bright blue sky. The air was filled with the sweet scent of apple blossom around them. Spinning around Jade could only see a small shack but no castle ruins. "How, can this be here? We are already in a different world than where we live. How come there is another world inside our magical world." asked Jade who was totally shocked by this. "Maybe our king will tell you when you get to see him." With that said, Pandar led the children down a gentle, grass covered slope with a few small cows and even a few sheep happily eating the grass. "Hello sweeties did you enjoy my milk?" came the voice of Bluebell one of the cows. "Yes. Thank you." Was the automatic answer before the children realized that there was another animal that could talk. "In our world we all can talk because we were born able to, but if you can't outside you can't here either. It was part of Merlin's spell."

An unexpected sound of horns being blown came across the land freezing the children and Sammy in their steps. "It's him, the king. He is coming." announced Pandar which encouraged all three of the children to quickly prepare themselves to be as presentable as they could possibly be ready for him. Even Sammy started cleaning and fluffing his tale and wiping down the front of his jumper.

From out of the distance appeared the king of the little people riding proudly on the back of a rat looking every bit the ruler, flanked by his guards on smaller mice and followed by a column of females dressed in all their finery. Coming to a halt in front of the children King Arthur the eighth as they were informed, climbed down from his transport and after straightening his bright red cloak and adjusting his jewel studded golden crown spoke. In a powerful and dominant voice that matched his regal position Arthur demanded to know why they had entered his land. Jade being the eldest stepped forward and curtsied before relayed to the king about the desperate situation over the danger of having her family's home knocked down as well as the animals' homes destroyed, unless they can find Mrs. West because only she might have the means to stop it. She also explained how they had heard about the little people from their good friend Ollie the owl but had sworn an oath not to ever share anything about what they know. "I know Ollie well." said the king "Does he still insist on reading a newspaper while he drinks his tea, and does he still watch over and help the animals, and wasn't it him who helped in the rescue of your father?". So many questions thought Jade intent on answering all. "Yes it is, He was a massive help to us." said Jade. "And he saved me when I was washed into the river." Squeaked up Sammy not wanting to be forgotten or left out. "What will you do if you find Mrs. West?" asked the king wanting to know what the children's plans were and so Jade repeated what she had already told to Pandar.

Happy with the children's story the king walked casually up to one of the little people that had accompanied him, and the two of them talked briefly before they returned to where Jade and the others were anxiously awaiting a decision from him. Addressing Jade the king said, "Here she is so tell her what you have told me and let her decide what or if to assist you." There was a surprising response from Jade as she said, "It can't be Mrs. West, she moved away from where she lived in our world long ago so why would she be here with you. I do not understand why". Standing only five inches high stood a slim female with straight greying black hair that went down to her shoulders, and wearing a full length dress with a roses design on. "I am Mrs. West. Let me explain to you."

came a response that the children were at first very skeptical of. None the less because of the many wondrous things that they had already seen and done since they first entered the land through the gardens magical arch, they all took a spot and sat down to listen to what she had to tell them. "Before I get started I must tell you that I can never return to your world if I do I will die." "Why would you die?" asked Asa. "In your world I have a deadly illness and am dying but here in this world and the one where Ollie lives I am not ill.", "Why are you so small here enquired Kaya inquisitively. "Like this I am just like the others and it helps me to help the needy here, plus I had a magic spell put on me. Now tell me about the trouble you are all in."

Over the next hour the children shared the troubles of themselves and of the animals, before turning their eyes onto Mrs. West hoping for some sort of miracle that would make everything right. During this time Kaya's eyes were occupied looking at as many of the female little people as she could in the hope of seeing wings on them. She was disappointed not to see fairies but accepted it and was given a new purpose, when one of the females informed her that there were fairies in her world and Sammy's too. Directing her attention to Sammy who had been sitting patiently at Asa's feet Mrs. west said," Once you get back to your world I want you to keep close to Ollie because you may be needed.", Then turning to face the children she told them to return home and all would be sorted for them. Feeling much better and more confident the children expressed their thanks to the king, Mrs. West and all of the others for their welcome and help before they left this magical world that was in a magical world. As they began to go Jade was approach by Mrs. West who whispered something into her ear. When asked what she had been told Jade just said, "It's a secret, you will have to be patient and trust me." Escorted by Pandar and a few warriors the children made their way back to the shack that they had entered the little peoples' realm through, pausing to say goodbye to their new secret friends before leaving this land.

Re-entering the dungeon Pandar again blew some powder over them that caused them to grow back to their original size, and then they were quickly joined by Sprinter who wanted to know all about where they had been and who they had seen. "There's another world there, it's beautiful and the king is very nice." said Kaya wanting to tell the news. "Sammy told me that he is on an important mission for the king before he left here. The last thing he said was that he will see you when you get back.". "Let's get going then, I want to know what Sammy is doing." said Asa clearly excited over what might be awaiting their return.

As they started walking back down the gentle slope that led away from the old ruins Kaya noted that none of them had seen Ollie, and wondered if he had also been sent on a mission by the king. "The last I heard he has gone to see his uncle again." Trying not to dwell on this the children and Sprinter casually continued homeward bound along the track way, back across the fields, past the shelter where they had spent a night before unaware that every step they took was being observed. It wasn't until they were about to leave the last field before Carters Brooke that Sprinter quietly whispered to Jade, "We had better be careful, many eyes are watching us". "Who's spying on us?" she asked without showing any sign of knowing. "I think that word has got out about what you have done and the animals want to get a look at you because you are heroes to them.

Travelling back downstream Jade was constantly looking around her for the watching animals. In the trees and overhead there were birds, over to her right was a herd of cows and to her left she could make out about a dozen rabbits and several field mice, wow we must be heroes to them all she thought to herself feeling very grown up while at the same time uneasy with so much attention on her. Turning back onto Carters Brooke they were met by Bushytail the girlfriend of Sammy who had been worried for him. "Is it true, is it true? Have you found a way to keep our homes safe, and did you really see the little people?" came the first of many questions for the group about their exploits. For Asa he couldn't resist telling the story of what they had done and where they had been, embellishing it with lots of skeletons and ghostly magic spells. The mention of that had Bushytail cowering behind Jade until Asa owned up and admitted to making the scary parts up to make it sound more exciting. After a little joking over this Jade suggested moving on so as to get back to the old barn and Ollie's home before night came. As the children and Sprinter continued home Sammy and Bushytail disappeared up into the foliage above.

After getting back to the old barn it was decided by Kaya that before going home they had to stop off and see Bernie and Dora, mainly to see their new babies but unfortunately for her the babies were still not to be seen. Now they had to see Ollie because Mrs. West had given Jade instructions on what else was to be done. On entering the barn, they were greeted by Ollie, Bernard the badger and an old friend Samuel the seagull who had heard about the threat they were all under. The children were over the moon to see their friends there to welcome them home, but this was not to be the end of the adventure yet.

Jade and Ollie went to one side so that they could talk about things. "I've been told exactly what is needed to be done. It will need your help." said Jade. "What do you want me to do for you asked Ollie eager to help. "Can you be here when we get back, there will be a very important thing that will need doing." said Jade, "But first I have to go home and see my daddy." Getting the others together she departed from her friends in the barn and led her brother and sister back across the field, along the mud pathway to the where the archway and their home was. Hurrying themselves into the house their mother Gloria surprised to see them come back in so quickly asked why they were back home so soon, because for her only a few minutes had passed by since they went out to play. Thinking fast Asa quickly said, "One of the pieces of wood in our tree house is broke so we want to ask daddy if he will fix it for us." "Kenneth! The children need your help with their tree house." shouted out Gloria to her husband who was busy studying a pile of documents concerning their home at that time.

Hearing the call about the tree house Kenneth knew that there must be a different reason why the children wanted him, and it had something to do with the land through the garden archway and it must be important. He knew that at that moment the children were indoors so he went to the hallway where his children were waiting for him. "Daddy, I know how you can stop the house being sold." "Don't tell me, you've been on another adventure." he said giving them a wink. "Yes we have and we found Mrs. West and she told me what to do." Sitting down on the stairs Kenneth listened intently as Jade spoke to her father. "Mrs. West told me what you have to do." "Okay what do I have to do?" asked Kenneth. "The bottom stair has a secret compartment under it, I was told how to open it but I want you to know before I open it." The two stood up and turned to face the stair in question and Jade took over while her father stood by hoping her mother wouldn't see what they were about to do.

Firstly, Jade knocked twice on the right side of it before repeating it on the left side and then again on the back of the stair. Just like a jack in the box a small wooden box about six inches by four inches sprang up from out of the stair. "That is amazing. You can open it." said Kenneth giving the honor for finding it to Jade. Carefully lifting the lid she saw a rolled up document inside. Handing it to her father she said, "Now I have to give it to Ollie so that he can deliver it to Mrs. West for whatever she wants it for, but she did tell me that we would all be happy for it". "Do you want me to come with you? You may need some help fixing it with Ollie?" asked Kenneth to which his daughter accepted.

Carefully choosing the right time Kenneth, carrying the document and Jade hurriedly entered the magical world and went straight to the barn and Ollie. "Hello there I am happy to see you." said Ollie as he adjusted his bi focal spectacles "Have you got any news for me?" "Yes, we found the document that we have to ask you to carry to the old ruins and give it to Pandar." said Jade to which "Yes I will, it will be my pleasure to." was the reply. Now all that needed doing was to find a way for Ollie to carry it as he was flying, Kenneth stepped in with a solution. "I can tie a ribbon around it so you can carry it in your claws" Once that was done they wished Ollie good luck with his task before watching him fly up into the sky and disappear into the distance.

Meanwhile in the ruined castle there was a lot of activity mixing the ingredients needed for some more magic powder learnt about from a book used by Merlin and passed down to the descendants of the ruling king or queen. King Arthur the eighth had given orders to his subjects to do whatever was wanted by Mrs. West, so she soon had them collecting the necessary plants needed for the concoction she was mixing. Because Ollie could fly faster than the children could run he reached the ruins during that night so he settled himself down to wait for the morning to come in the hope that somebody would come out to him. The next morning, he was disturbed by the sound of the scampering of little feet so he studied the area before his eyes locked on to a little man and he knew who it was. "Pandar I'm here now and have something for you from the children that Mrs. West requires." called down Ollie from a hole high up in the wall where a window once was. "Good I will tell her you have arrived." shouted back Pandar trying to talk loud enough to be heard by Ollie before scampering off again.

Down through the dungeon passed the skeletons, skulls and the rusty swords he went back outside of the shack to the little people's realm, where a group of little the people with their king and Mrs. West were anxiously waiting. "Tell me Lizzy do you think that those children and squirrel can be trusted not to tell anybody about us." asked Arthur the eighth. "Ollie trusted them enough to help in the rescue their father and bring him home." replied Mrs. West. Knowing this eased the king's fears about outsiders being aware of not only that they did know about them, but also that they knew how to enter the little people's world. He could well remember the childhood stories about the cruelty of the invaders and Merlin's magic spell to keep them safe. I'm just being paranoid he thought to himself and that eased when from out of the shack emerged Pandar carrying a giant roll of thick paper.

Pandar handed the rolled up paper to the king who opened it out and studied what it had to say. He then looked at Mrs. West for her acknowledgement before shrinking it down to a better size for them. "Now sign what you need to and I'll return it to the correct size. That way you can let Pandar return it and we can go back to being a mystery to the outsiders." commanded the king. Using a feather from a bird of prey she dipped it into some ink and signed her name on the bottom of the paper, before the king uttered out the spell that would return it to its original size.

Mrs. West helped Pandar re-roll the paper and tied it, before helping to lift it so that he could take it back through the shack and the dungeon for Ollie.

Being heavy for someone the size of the little people, Pandar's face was quite red and his hair was dripping with sweat from the struggle he had to endure in getting there. As he got into the great hall ruins Ollie flew down from high up in the wall to welcome him back. "The king has instructed me to tell you that he has allowed this because he does not want any of the animals to suffer, and he was impressed by the actions of the children in their willingness to help." said Pandar. "Thank you and that goes for all of us." said Ollie as he picked up the rolled up paper and rose back up into the sky.

Having been entrusted to carry the paper both ways to and from the ruins gave him a feeling of being indispensable, but he knew that Samuels's web feet prevented him from doing it so it was left to him. As it was Ollie was already considered vital to them by most of the animals because of his wisdom and ability to organize things.

Ollie had barely flown half way back when he saw Samuel flying toward him. "Too wit to woo Hello Samuel, have you come to meet me or is there a problem at home I need to be made aware of?" he asked "No problems at the barn. Everyone is waiting to welcome you back." squawked Samuel as he flew into a position at Ollie's side." Flying side by side Ollie was able to tell his friend about everything that had happened and what was being done now. There was a great sense of success for them but they did not know that at home a gang of wickedly nasty animals were planning to prevent them from saving all of their homes, led by Spatey the fat cat who was bitter about being chased off by Sprinter. There was also Wiley the weasel, Slimy the snake and Ronald the rat all easily controlled by the cat.

Back at the barn there was a cheer from the children and Kenneth when they saw the two birds flying over the field next to the one that the barn was in. Quickly they cleared a big space on the ground for them to land on, looking forward to their return and the eagerly awaited explanation as to why this rolled up paper was so important to them. Kenneth got all the animals concerned to gather in the middle of the space where Ollie and Samuel had landed so that he could tell them all at the same time. By this time Ollie had returned to his place up on the wall and Sprinter had gone to where Bernie lived so as to bring him to the barn.

Once they had all gathered Kenneth addressed them, "As you know my children with the help of a few of you have been in search of Mrs. West and the little people.". "They don't exist you fool." came a critical voice from the back belonging to Bernard the grumpy badger. "That's where you are wrong. We found them." answered Asa in defense of his father. "Thank you my son." said his proud father before continuing, "Yes they did find them and thanks to them was able to see Mrs. West. She told jade my eldest where to find a document proving our house and the land where you all live belong to her." "What's that got to do with us?" asked Bernard not fully realizing the meaning of this. Kenneth then looked directly at him and continued with what he was saying before being so rudely interrupted. "With the help of some magic provided by King Arthur the Eight's little people, Mrs. West has signed over the ownership to myself on the condition that the land covered by the document be left as it is with access only with our permission and ownership must stay in my family." This news was more than welcomed by all of the animals because they need not fear their homes being destroyed.

Now Kenneth had to have all this recorded with Mr. Simpson who had to be informed that the land that he wanted to sell was not his to sell, which meant leaving his ever increasing number of animal friends to return through the archway to his real world. For the children, they were in no hurry to go back yet so Kaya suggested visiting Bernie and Dora to see their young ones. They were in deed lucky on this day as it was to be the first time that they were to leave the place where Dora had been caring for them, and it was to be their first contact with others. With that done it was time for them to leave this magical land and return home and remove the for sale sign from the entrance to the magical world. As they walked through the archway the usual flash of bright light was barely a flicker which to the children meant that their access to the magical world was closing behind them again. Kaya reminded her brother and sister how it was closed before and the animals reopened it for them when needed so who knew it might again. The following morning Kenneth went into Newton Priory and made sure that everyone that had to know was informed that the house and wooded area were legally his families until such time as Mrs. West wanted it back. In a way his family was custodians of Mrs. West's home and land and would always protect it and their animal friends from danger. Soon enough that danger would come to arise but that is a story yet untold.

www.ingramcontent.com/pod-product-compliance
Lightning Source LLC
Chambersburg PA
CBHW071842190726
48292CB00005B/1871